ISLANDS OF THE SUNSET

In the days of long ago,
there was once a King
of the Blue Islands.

The King was an old man.

He had always lived on the Blue Islands.

The Blue Islands lay far away
across the sea.

There were trees on the Islands,
and rocks on the golden sand
by the deep blue sea.

There were flowers under the trees.

There were blue flowers
and yellow flowers,
red flowers and white flowers.

All day, the sun shone down
on the trees and the flowers,
on the golden sands and the sea.

There was a big hill
on the biggest island,
and the King lived in a castle
on the very top of the hill.

The King's son was dead,
but he had a grandson,
and this boy
was now the Prince of the Islands.

Every day, as the sun set,
the Prince looked out across the sea.

Far away, across the sea,
there were three islands.

Every day, as the sun set,
the sea shone like gold.

The three islands were called
the Islands of the Sunset.

One day, the Prince went down
to the sands by the sea.

There was an old sailor on the sands.
He was looking out to sea.

The Prince went up to the old sailor.

" Sailor," said the Prince.
" Do you know the islands
we can see far away ?"

" Yes," said the sailor. " I sailed
to the Islands of the Sunset long ago,
when I was a boy.
I went there to look for gold."

" Did you find it ?" asked the Prince.

" Yes," said the old sailor.

" Long, long ago the Black Pirates
lived on the Islands of the Sunset.
They were bad pirates,
and they had sacks and sacks of gold.
They took the gold from ships sailing by,
and they killed the sailors.

The Black Pirates left the Islands
long ago, but the gold is still there,
if you know where to look for it."

The Prince looked out across the sea
to the far islands.
The sky was red in the setting sun,
and the red in the sky
shone red on the sea.

"I will ask the King for a ship, and
sail to the Islands of the Sunset," he said.
"Will you go with me, old sailor?"
"Yes, I will go," said the old sailor.
"You will never find the gold,
if I do not go with you."
The next day the Prince went
to the King.

" May I have a ship ?" he asked.

" What do you want with a ship ?" asked the King.

" I want to sail to the Islands of the Sunset, to find gold," said the Prince.

" I have met an old sailor.
He knows the Islands,
and he knows that gold is hidden there."

" I have always lived in the Blue Islands," said the King. " I do not want gold.
But you may have a ship,
and sailors to sail with you.

But when you have seen the Islands of the Sunset, come back to the Blue Islands, whether you find gold or not."

" I will come back," said the Prince.

The next day, the King went
down to the sea with the Prince.
There was the ship,
and the sailors were setting the sails.
The sun shone on the blue sea.
The Prince went onto the ship.

The wind sang in the white sails,
and the ship sailed away across the sea.
The wind blew, and the ship sailed well,
and when the sun set in the sea,
they were not far
from the Islands of the Sunset.

The next day, the ship sailed nearer
and nearer to the Islands.

The Prince looked at the Islands
as the ship came in.

The old sailor was with him.

"The Islands look like black rocks,"
said the Prince.
"There are no trees there."

"No," said the old sailor.
"There are no trees
on the Islands of the Sunset.
There are no trees, and no flowers,
and no grass on these Islands."

There were rocks in the sea,
and the ship came in by the rocks.
The Prince took three sailors,
and the old sailor with him,
and went onto the island.

They went up into the hills,
to look for gold.

It was very hot
on the Islands of the Sunset.
The sun shone down,
and the black rocks got hotter
and hotter in the sunshine.
The old sailor led the way
up into the hills.
It took them a long time, in the hot sun,
but they went on and on.

Then, in the side of the hill,
they saw a cave.

"Look!" said the old sailor.
"Long ago, the Black Pirates
lived in that cave.

If there is still gold on the island,
we shall find it in the cave."

The Prince and the sailors
came to the cave, and looked in.
It was very black in the cave,
as they went in, out of the sunshine.

" The gold will be under the rocks at
the back of the cave," said the old sailor.

There were big rocks
at the back of the cave.

They looked under the rocks,
but there was no gold there.

They were just coming out,
when the Prince saw another little cave,
in the side of the big cave.

" Look !" he said. " What is there ?"

It was very black in the little cave, but
they could just see something by a rock.

It was a sack!

The sailors pulled the sack out
into the big cave.

There were three other sacks near it.

They pulled them all out.

The Prince looked in the sacks.

" Gold !" he said. " We have found it."

" We have found the Black Pirates' gold !"

The old sailor saw something
under the rock. He pulled it out.
It was a knife.

" Look !" he said.

" This knife was near the gold.
It has not been here long.
It is a Black Pirate's knife.
The Black Pirates must have come back
to the Islands of the Sunset.
We must get back to the ship.
If the Black Pirates find us here,
they will kill us all."

" We will take the gold with us,"
said the Prince.

They took the sacks with them
back to the ship.

The sun was hot on the black rocks,
and it was a long way back to the ship.

They got there when the sun had just set.

" We cannot sail now,"
said the old sailor.

" There are rocks in the sea
by these islands."

" We will sail as soon as it is day,"
said the Prince.

They set sail the next day,
as soon as the sun was up.

" We will sail back to the Blue Islands,"
said the Prince.
" We have found the gold,
and we will take it back to the King."

They had just pulled out from the rocks,
and were setting out
for the Blue Islands,
when they saw another ship,
not far away.

It was a black ship,
with black sails and a black flag.

" The Black Pirates !" said the old sailor.
" The Black Pirates !"
We must get away.
The Black Pirates will kill us all !"

The wind blew,
and the little ship sailed well.

The Prince looked back.
The black ship looked bigger.

" The Black Pirates are getting nearer,"
he said.

" Set more sails !" said the old sailor.

" We cannot sail as fast as they can,"
said the Prince. " They are coming nearer."

" We must !" said the old sailor.
" We must get away !"

But the black ship
with the black sails sailed nearer
and nearer and nearer.

The Prince could see the pirates
on the ship now. Each pirate had a knife.

The Prince looked across the sea.
Far away across the sea
he could just see the Blue Islands.

Nearer to the ship, he saw a big rock.
It was so big,
that it was a little island.
The ship was sailing by.

" Take the ship to that rock !"
said the Prince.

" Take the ship in, very near to the rock.
We have just time.
We will put the gold on the rock.
Perhaps the Black Pirates will stop
for the gold."

The sea was deep by the rock,
and the sailors took the ship in.

They shook out the gold,
and tossed the sacks onto the rock.
The gold fell out.

It shone on the rock in the sunshine.

The Prince looked back.

The Black Pirates were very near now.

The Prince's ship pulled away
from the rock.

The Black Pirates' ship came on.

On and on it came.

It was near the rock now:

The gold on the rock shone
in the sunshine.

Then one of the Black Pirates saw
what was on the rock.

" Gold !" he called out. " Gold !"

The ship pulled in towards the rock.

The Black Pirates left the ship,
and went down onto the rock
for the gold.

The gold lay there in the sunshine.

It was all over the top of the rock.

The Prince's ship was sailing well.
The wind blew,
and the little ship sailed on, across the sea
towards the Blue Islands.

The rock was a long way away,
when the Prince next looked back.

He could just see the Black Pirates' ship.
It was still at the rock.

The little ship sailed on,
and as the sun set in the sea,
they came to the Blue Islands.
The Prince left the ship,
and went up the hill to the castle,
to find the King.

The King came down the hill to meet him.

" You have come back !" said the King.
" You have come back to the Blue Islands!"

" Yes, I have come back," said the Prince.

" Did you find the gold?"
asked the King.

" Yes, we found the gold,"
said the Prince.
" But we saw the Black Pirates,
and we left it for them,
so that we could get away."

The King looked out across the sea.

" There is our gold," he said.

The sun had set,

but the sky still shone gold,

and the gold in the sky shone

like gold on the sea.

" Come," said the King,

and they went into the castle.